Long Line Rider

By

B. G. Priest

Long Line Rider
Copyright©2015 B.G. Priest

ACKNOWLEDGMENTS

For my family: Debra, April, Roseanne, Amanda and
Bobbie Jean

Contents

CHAPTER ONE

The Mess

The dawn came early as Luke stirred from a conscious sleep. The sounds filtering into his head told him something wasn't right, and he should get to moving, get to his feet, do something goddamn it, and not just lay there and be a dumb son-of-a-bitch. Dumb sons-a-bitches tended to run in Luke's bloodline, but no one ever accused him of being dumb. Stupid- maybe, but not dumb.

Dumb, stupid or what the hell ever, Luke's subconscious took over, and his body began to roll to the edge of his bed, and his feet found the floor.

Stumbling over to the window and easing back the curtain, Luke found himself looking out at the hulking body of the one and only Mississippi County Sheriff, Moss Brown... and Sheriff Brown was heading toward the front door with that (deputy Fife looking dude) Deputy Jimmie Jack Johnson in tow. Not being able to fully process what was going on in his hungover head, Luke blinked his eyes trying to focus, and made a stumbling dash to gather up his britches and get 'em on before the Sheriff got to knocking down the door, as he was sometimes prone to do.

Luke made it to the door just as the big sheriff laid the first knock with his big ol' meat hook knuckles.

Opening the door and squinting at the unusually bright morning sun, Luke stared into the round, red, sweaty, porcine face of the old sheriff.

"What's up sheriff?" Luke asked. Sheriff Brown stood with both hands on the door frame and kinda looked around the darkened room through his Aviators seemingly un-impressed, and stepped inside with Jimmie Jack almost stuck up his ass.

"Zat your automobile out there sonny boy?" glancing back over his shoulder in the direction of the shiny little gold colored Corvair convertible sitting in Luke's yard.

"Well, naw, it ain't mine, but I am driving it sheriff," Luke replied in his good-ol-boy Arkansas accent with a hint of a nervous smile across his lips. "Why, is there a problem?"

The big man stepped into the room and put that big palm upside Luke's forehead and led him backwards toward an overstuffed imitation leather recliner where Luke managed to un-ceremoniously plop down. "You might say they is a problem boy. Now you wanna tell me who that auto-mo-bile belongs to?"   "Uh, yeah, it belongs to Tiny Hargett. Why, is there a problem sheriff? We was drinking and shootin' a little pool down at the Rebel Club in Luxora last night, and Tiny met up with a girl and he took off with her and tossed me the keys and said he'd be pickin' it up later."

Sheriff Brown took the old fedora off his balding head and slowly wiped a snot stained handkerchief across his dripping brow.

"Zat right?" Sheriff Brown asked, almost accusatory in tone. Luke didn't like the feel of this at all. "Uh huh," Luke nodded. "Is there a problem?" he repeated.

"Well boy, like I said, they is a problem, and it involves you and that car out there. We found your buddy Tiny this mornin'… and let me tell you boy… he's deader'n a doornail! "But I'm thinkin' you already knew that, didn't you?"

Luke tried to absorb what the big man had just thrown at him. Did he just say Tiny was dead? How could that be? His best friend in the whole wide world, friends since second grade.

Luke's brain was calling bullshit! "Must be some mistake!" he reasoned. "What happened Sheriff? How… how did he die?" "Well now, that's what me and you gonna talk about down at my office sonny boy. We gonna git this shit figured out purty damn quick… I can promise you *that* much!"

Moss Brown then turned his attention to his deputy. "Git on the horn and have George git down here and tow that car down to the impound. Oh, and tell him to make it pronto! I don't need no bullshittin' around with this!" "Yes sir Sheriff, I'm on it." Jimmy left the house headed toward the sheriff's cruiser to use the radio.

Now, old George Miller ran a local garage and salvage yard, and was the county's go to guy when it came to hauling impounds and such.

A few years back, Luke had set up a portable building business and had been looking for some chat gravel to spread out on the lot to make it easier to walk and drive on. At some point, he had mentioned this fact to Tiny and Tiny told him about a big ol' pile of gravel sitting on the side of route 61 just north of town, Said the county had put it there just for folks like Luke, and that he should just head up there and help himself to all he needed.

Well, to make a long story short, Luke did go up there and started helping himself to a load of that gravel, and in hindsight, if he had paid better attention to the sign someone had stuck in the middle of that mountain of gravel that read: "PROPERTY OF THE STATE OF ARKANSAS" he would *not* have wound up in the back of that patrol car with his hands cuffed together, and would *not* have had to pay an attorney three hundred and forty dollars to get him out of stealing seventy five dollars worth of gravel, and *that* gravel would *not* have ended up filling the potholes in George Miller's parking lot! And, *if* you wish in one hand and shit in the other…just see which one fills up the quickest!

" Okay boy, git you some clothes on. We got some more talking to do" Moss ordered.

Back at the sheriff's office, Moss Brown tosses the fedora on a chair as he and Luke get comfortable in the interrogation room. He offers Luke a smoke, which he readily accepts, and reaches across the table with the Zippo and lights him up.

"Now, let's get down to business son. You say you was with Tiny last night, and he took off with some gal and told you to take his car?" "That's right, Luke replied. You gonna tell me what happened to Tiny? How was he killed?" "Whoa there little fella. First thing you got to understand is, this here's my investigation. I'm the one askin' the questions you got that?" the sheriff answered with more than a hint of indignity. "Now, do you own a gun, boy?" "No sir I don't. I aint had a gun in over two years." "What about a knife, or say, a machete?" "Yeah, I got a huntin' knife, and a pocket knife. You saying Tiny was murdered? Cut up?" Luke continued to ask. "I'm sayin,' I'm still the one askin' the questions here boy, and don't you start testin' my patience. Now then, let me ask you this… where is your knife?" "I don't know; I guess it's in my truck." Brown fixes Luke with a hard stare, then reaches into his own shirt pocket and pulls out a five-inch Carter folding knife. "This your knife son?' the sheriff asked. "Yeah that's mine. What you doing with it? "You get it outta my truck?" "Nope," the sheriff said matter-of-factly. "The coroner pulled it out of Tiny Joe's nut sack!"

"What? I don't know how it would have got there sheriff. I swear to you I didn't do nothing to Tiny." Luke was emphatic.

It was just beginning to sink in to Luke that his best friend *was* dead, and it was becoming uncomfortably obvious that he was the number one suspect.

"You are telling me one thing boy, and this here sticker is telling me something else. I done had this knife looked at, and your prints is all over it, along with your buddy's blood! Now, to me that represents a purty big problem for you. Now why don't you tell me where you went after you all left the Rebel Club." "First off, there wasn't no "you all" to it sheriff. I left the club by myself and went straight to my place and went to sleep. Didn't wake up till I heard you pull up this morning. That's the God's honest truth!" "Did anybody see you leave the club by yourself?" Brown asked. "Everybody there should have seen Tiny leave with that girl before I left. Just ask Jake, he was bartending last night. He should be able to back me up." "I found a book of matches on Tiny…a book of matches from The Rebel Club, and I did ask Jake. I woke him up before daylight this mornin' and he said he remembered seeing you leave just a few minutes after Tiny." "Naw, that aint right. He's just confused an' all. Had to been at least an hour after they left when I did. There was a dozen other people in there. Somebody *had* to know when I left." "You just look here boy, I aint gonna waste my time tracking all them folks down and windin' up with the same story Jake told. Fact is, I got enough on you already, and if you don't come up with a good story now, I'm gonna lock your ass up and let the prosecutor have at it!"

Brown's agitation was beginning to show now and he was getting red in the face and sweating profusely again. "Son, them two was flat ass butchered, and I think you know more than you're talkin' about!" "Two? What do you mean two? Was it Tiny *and* the girl, sheriff?" "Hell yeah, it was both of 'em. Tiny damn near had his head cut off and your knife in his nuts, and the girl had her throat slashed too right along with her cootchie.! Seems to me that "whoever" did it, and I'm sure thinkin' it was you, had a might big grudge against Tiny and/or that gal. You wanna tell me who that girl is son?" "I swear to God Almighty sheriff, I don't know that girl, I don't know where they went, and I aint never seen her before!"

Brown just stared at Luke out of exasperation.... or was it just disappointment.

After tapping an ink pen on the table top for what seemed like hours instead of the seconds that actually transpired, Moss pushed himself away from the table and slowly stood up.

"I want to believe you son," Brown said quietly, "but you aint givin' me much and this here thing don't seem to be goin' your way. I'm gonna have to hold you and turn this case over to the prosecutor...let him decide how it's gonna go. Now, if you think of something else or...if you just wanna get something off your chest, well...well you just let me know. In the meantime, Luke I'm gonna have to hold you here on charges of double homicide, and they aint no automatic bail on that kind of charge so you gonna have to see a judge for an arraignment and bail hearing."

It all started to sink in now for Luke, he really was being charged for the murder of his friend and that girl and he didn't care for these developments at all!

The next morning, after spending a long and sleepless night in the county jail, Luke was walked across the street to the county courthouse where he had a quick arraignment in front of a county judge where he was promptly and officially charged with two counts of first degree murder with aggravating circumstances and bond was denied.

That judge ordered him back in one month for a preliminary hearing and also found him eligible for a public defender.

CHAPTER TWO

Judgement

"All rise!" the bailiff ordered. "Please be seated. This is the third day of July, nineteen hundred and sixty-seven, and this is a preliminary hearing in the case of the State of Arkansas versus Luther Dee Price. Mister Prosecutor, will you give us the background in this case?" Judge Kline queried.

"Yes your Honor, this is the case of the people versus one Luther Dee Price. Mr. Price is accused of two counts of first degree homicide, and the State intends to seek the death penalty in this case, as the Sate believes this is a heinous and premeditated double murder with aggravating circumstances and is worthy of capital punishment."

The prosecutor was one Marshal James Port and came from one of the more prominent families in Mississippi County. Born of privilege, raised with a silver spoon; but that silver spoon these days is used more often than not to deliver a little spit of cool white powder to the young Mr. Port's nostrils.

Now, Judge Sylvester Kline is a dog of a different pack. Judge Kline brought to the bench an un-deniable legal virtue that would make Sister Theresa look like a ten-dollar back alley whore. Although the Judge was a judicious and efficient man, his overpowering (and sometimes over indulged) sense of fairness in the legal world, caused a lot of folks to do a lot of time in cases that might have had a different outcome in a different court with a different judge. Judge Kline earned the moniker "hanging judge" and he wore the badge with undeniable pride and distinction.

Now seems like a good time to talk about our hero's defense attorney:

Ronnie Ball took to the law like a snowball takes to sunshine. Ronnie would rather have been an auto mechanic as he would a lawyer, but to appease his parents, and especially his daddy, who was himself a graduate of the University of Arkansas School of Law over at Fayetteville, Ronnie reluctantly applied for the law school program there, and to his dismay was actually accepted.

Not saying Ronnie wasn't a decent litigator when the notion hit him… he applied himself to the best of his ability and did manage to graduate ninety second out of a class of ninety nine, and did manage to pass the bar exam after only three tries; it's just that in the overall scheme of things, Ronnie was just a kind of "laid back" guy. After all, a good cold brew and a thin-crust jalapeno and pepperoni pizza was better than motions and briefs any old day!

"Mr. Ball? Is your client prepared to enter a plea?" the Judge asked. "Yes we are your Honor."

"Very well then, Mr. Price, you are charged with two counts of first degree murder, which in the state of Arkansas with aggravating circumstance is a capital offense, and it brings with it the possibility of the death penalty. Do you understand these charges against you?"

Luke stood facing the judge, still not *really* understanding exactly how he got to this point in his life, but he did have a modicum of belief that he would get out of this predicament, that as they say, justice will prevail, and sweet Jesus, he hoped like hell it would.

"I plead *not* guilty your Honor!" Luke couldn't help but put a little extra emphasis on NOT!

11

"Very well, the court accepts your plea and sets your trial date for... ok, we'll set this for trial at 8:am on September 20, 1967. Mr. Price, we'll see you back here at that time."

Luke sat in his cell brooding most of the time. The only breaks in the monotony came when the jailers brought the slop or his legal mail. Occasionally his attorney Ronnie Ball would come by to touch base on some evidence or go over testimony with his client. Had to make sure they were on the same page and all. Ball would ask him things like: Was he sure he went straight home that night or, did he know of anyone who would want to do any harm to Tiny or, try to imagine how Luke's knife got stuck in Tiny if he didn't stick it there.

"For crying out loud," Luke said to himself," what the hell am I missing here? The only thing they really got on me is that goddamned knife and the fact that I had his car. Shit fire! I didn't give a big fuck 'bout who he was screwing; long as it wasn't my gal,' or, ex gal he mused. Hell, Leslie quit talking to him just a couple days after the murders. "Guess she didn't have much faith in me anyway," he thought.

They said Tiny and that girl, Mindy was the name that he had first heard in court, was found out on Barfield Landing at the Mississippi River. Barfield Landing was a local hangout where couples and party animals usually went when the bars closed. It was a good secluded place away from town to start a good bonfire and sit around and swap bullshit stories, or try to run your hand down your girl's blouse before she came to her senses and slapped dog-shit out of you.

They also told him Mindy was married and, that, in Luke's mind, opened up the possibility of a motive for the scorned husband to kill the unfaithful little filly. But then again Ronnie Ball had said they checked the old boy out and that he had a solid alibi... something about being on the river barge where he was working when the murders took place.

Once again, Luke worked out in his own mind, just about *any* alibi could be phonied up. Yep, this would need a little more looking in to.

The jailer, just a kid really, brought Luke's dinner in to him on a slow, boring Sunday afternoon, and our boy Luke was waiting for him with more questions.

"How's it going Billy?" Luke asked. "Awright I guess. How you doing Luke?" "Thinkin' 'bout goin' out for a beer. You wanna come?" Luke asked with that sly grin. "Naw...guess I better stick around here." Billy replied with with his own sheepish smile. "Hey you know what Billy? I been thinkin'; you happen to know that old boy's name, you know, the one who was married to that girl that got killed?" "Uhhh, yeah, yeah his name is Buddy, Buddy Wright. What you wanna know for?" "Aw, I just kinda been thinking about it...about my case n' all. You know anything about him?" "Nah, not much, except he's from over in Osceola. Been in trouble before. Hell, he's been in here a couple of times, fightin' n' such. I guess he fancies himself a Billy-badass or somethin'. ". As a matter of fact, he's on his way back to Cummins for parole violation. Guess he's gotta finish out a three year bit on an assault charge. Looks like you'll get a chance to see 'em before too long Luke." Luke didn't really want to hear anything like that. "Damn Billy, you already got me convicted?" Luke quipped. "Oh no, nothin' like that Luke. You don't seem like you'd do anything like that, but word has it you aint got much of a defense an' all and, well you know..." Billy replied almost apologetically

"Yeah, yeah I know. I aint got much to work with and all. No good alibi and not much of a lawyer neither. But I tell you what Billy; I do have the truth on my side." Luke tried hard to believe his own words, but it was getting tough just hanging on to that thread.

13

"Well, look here Luke; I gotta get back to cleaning the Sheriff's office. I'll holler at you later ok?" Luke dropped his head as the young jailer turned to leave. "Awright Billy, see you later."

September 20th came pretty damned slow from Luke's point of view, but trial day was here and Luke was looking forward to getting' the hell out of that stinkin' ass jail cell, even if it did mean either going home, or going to prison. Preferably home!

Luke was sitting in the holding cell at the courthouse when Ronnie Ball came in and sat down beside him. Ronnie had a curious look about him as he shuffled his papers and finally turned his attention back to Luke.

"Luke? The prosecutor has made an offer in your case. It seems he knows they don't have a whole lot of evidence against you, but what they have is fairly compelling and he is willing to proceed IF you don't accept this offer. I think that with what we have, it's about the best we can hope for right now."

"For God's sake Ronnie, spit it out!" Luke was getting a little impatient with the hum-hawing around. "Ok, ok. They're offering second degree, two counts, with a chance of parole after twenty."

Ronnie searched Luke's face for some sign of life. He saw Luke's expression and felt for him. "Goddamn Ronnie," Luke said in a somber and un-believing tone, "Twenty years? For something I didn't do? Luke grasped Ronnie's arm and looked in his eyes hard like.

"What the hell? What the *HELL* Ronnie? I don't know...I...um, well, what would you do if it was you?" his voice softer now. "I gotta tell you Luke, it's the best we got right now. I think you should take it. We can't appeal on a plea deal, but I'll keep workin' it. I believe you didn't do this Luke. I'll keep workin' it and get some answers.... I promise."

Luke looked down toward the floor. He believed Ronnie would try... but fuck! Twenty years?

Still looking down, softly he said, "Alright…I'll take it.

CHAPTER THREE

NEW DIGS

On October 1, 1967, Luke was led from the county jail where he had languished for the past three months, to a Mississippi County Sheriffs car to be driven down to the Pine Bluff Unit of the Arkansas Department of Corrections.

In those days, there were two main prison farms in Arkansas, and the diagnostic unit at Pine Bluff which was adjacent to and part of the boys' reformatory. The oldest of the prisons was the Cummins Unit, established in 1912, and was essentially just a big farm worked by inmates.

The second one was the Tucker Unit about fifty miles away that was started around 1920, but both were run by one man. They called him Big Jim, but his real name was James Byrton; and nobody fucked with Big Jim Byrton.

Big Jim originally hailed from Marion County up in north central Arkansas where it is said that he killed a man up there for foolin' around with one of his moonshine stills. Now whether Jim killed the fellow for messing with his still or for messing with Big Jim's woman as some folks believed, it is still a matter of contention, but suffice it to say that Jim was a very bad man and *never* lost his propensity to do significant harm to his fellow human beings.

Anyway, Jim wound up leaving Marion County around 1929 in a bit of a hurry, and relocated down to Pine Bluff and took a job at the Pine Bluff Industrial School for Boys as a guard.

There are quite a few men still around that did time at PBIS and each and every one of them would tell you that Big Jim was a special kind of son-of-a-bitch! He took an unusual amount of pleasure administering corporal punishment which he doled out with a leather strap he lovingly referred to as "OL' Blister". A lot of those men still carry scars from that strap and the deeper kind of scars that clothes cannot cover up.

Big Jim came up through the ranks pretty quickly, and after about three years was installed as the superintendent of the school where he continued to enjoy overseeing punishment sessions with Ol' Blister as the main attraction.

Around about 1934, Big Jim managed to wrangle himself in as Superintendent of Prisons, and was put in charge of Cummins and Tucker, where he promptly set himself up as king and emperor of the farms.

Graft, intimidation, murder, and intimidation were the order of the day down there and nothing happened without Jim's say so. Big Jim got very rich off the backs of Arkansas' inmates, and padding the pockets of the bigwigs up in Little Rock insured that Jim would be around for quite some time.

One of the first things Jim implemented was the use of inmates as guards. It was a sound plan from Jim's perspective. It cut down on overhead and instilled in the inmates a fear that precluded most of them from getting any ideas about running off.

Jim Byrton sent out an edict to his inmate guards that went something like this: If they caught any inmates trying, or even thinking about escape, the inmate guard had the authority to kill that inmate, and that inmate guard, known as a Long Line

Rider, (because they rode horses and carried carbine rifles) would get special privileges for carrying out the killing.

Those privileges could include such things as alcohol, women, furloughs and even their own private houses on the farm. And many of the Riders took full advantage of the perks offered.

The ride down to Pine Bluff was quiet and mostly uneventful. Generally small talk with the deputy and watching the countryside fly by... bean fields and cotton fields seemed to stretch on forever with only the occasional hamlet or small town to drive through.

It is only 160 miles from Mississippi County to Pine Bluff, but to Luke it seemed like a thousand. With every mile they traveled he was getting farther from the things he was familiar with and the people he knew and the places he went.

Not that Luke was a wallflower by any stretch of the imagination, he certainly wasn't opposed to a little carousing and mildly misguided adventuring, but he did prefer the simpler things in life, like sitting on the banks of a good fishing hole and dipping his toes in the cooling water on a stifling hot Delta summer day. Or, his momma's biscuits. Oh yes, those wonderful fluffy little catheads. We're talking melt in your mouth, soppin' good! Even if he wasn't in the mess he was in now, he wouldn't ever get to sample those biscuits again, and that made him sad.

His mom had passed in '65 from a stroke only two years after his dad had died from complications from pneumonia. After his parents, that left Luke with his two sisters, Pam and Betty.

Both the girls, one older and one younger than he, had taken up with airmen stationed at Blytheville Air Force Base, and were starting and raising their families in the four corners of the world.

Pam and her two kids were stationed in some "Bad" place in Germany. Not that it was a bad place at all according to Pam, it's just that the name of the town they lived in was called

Badneuhaus or Badnaightwas or something like that, Luke couldn't remember.

Betty, who was expecting her first baby, was on some island way out in the Pacific, and by her accounts it was a miserable little island, hot, humid, and not much to do.

Luke would give just about anything right now to be on that island.

The diagnostics unit at Pine Bluff was Luke's first taste of prison life and it didn't take him long to figure out that he didn't like it at all.

The purpose, or purposes of first sending an inmate to diagnostics was so that they could do preliminary medical and psychological exams, haircuts, orientation and decide where the inmates would best fit into the system. Oddly enough, Jim Byrton did not technically have anything to do with the diagnostic unit or have anything to say about what went on there… well, at least not officially that is. But, un-officially, Jim's tentacles reached into that part of the system as well. He made sure that he had the administrator of the unit and many of the officers staffed there under his control. That way, he could get the inmates placed where *he* wanted them.

At that time, in the mid to late sixties, Arkansas was in the early stages of expanding the Department of Corrections with new prisons planned for Varner, Saline County, and Calico Rock.

As it turns out, crime was becoming big business in Arkansas and Big Jim had his sights set on being the top dog. Little did he know, there were forces in Little Rock that had no intentions of letting that happen. In some circles, Jim Byrton was considered a dinosaur and a throwback to times that progressives wanted to see sent to extinction.

When Luke got to the diagnostic unit he was led down a broad hallway where he was told to get in a line of six other incoming inmates where they were given a yellow jumpsuit and a bedroll with a plastic covered pillow, blanket and a sheet.

Next, the men were led to showers where they were ordered to strip, bend over and cough for a corrections officer who seemed to be as dis-interested in his work as any man Luke had ever seen, and who wouldn't be after looking up men's' asses all day.

The other guys didn't talk much, Luke figured they were as happy to be there as he was. Wasn't any use in trying to make "friends" as they were not going to be staying there but for a couple of days.

Those two days went buy surprisingly quick from Luke's point of view and before he knew it he was being shackled and cuffed and loaded into an old white painted school bus all by himself, with "Arkansas Dept. of Corrections" stenciled on its sides, for the forty-minute drive to his new home Tucker Prison Farm.

As the bus pulled of Highway 65 onto prison property outside the little hamlet of Grady, Arkansas, it was coming up on 10:am and it was blazing hot even at this late time of the year. Luke could see heat waves dancing off the cotton fields and could make out big red tractors kicking up dust in the distance.

The road to the prison sally port was nothing more than a broad, dusty gravel road but was meticulously graded as if they were expecting royal guest at any time. Luke was pretty sure the road wasn't graded in his honor.

As the bus came to a stop in front of a massive barbed wire gate adjacent to a looming guard tower, a cloud of dust caught up and enveloped it.

Looking past the wire fence Luke could see three or four low roofed metal buildings that he estimated were about 100feet by 200feet each. He surmised these must be the dormitories, and off to the left stood what appeared to be some sort of pavilion with solid walls halfway up and the upper part of the openings screened in with big canvas curtains rolled up over the openings. There were rows of tables and benches inside that told Luke this must be the chow hall. Luke could see four or five men milling about inside wearing white uniforms. In fact, all the men he could see, whether in the chow hall or on a passing tractor, or out on the yard were in white except for two guys standing beside horses that were tied to the fence about seventy-five yards away.

They had on white britches, but their shirts were colored, like street clothes, and they had on cowboy hats, cowboy boots and were holding on to what looked like carbine rifles.

As Luke stepped from the bus, he noticed the two men were staring him down hard through their mirrored Aviator sunglasses.

"What you got there?" A booming voice called from above. The question came from another cowboy dressed figure up in the guard tower. "Mississippi County. Got you a new one." the officer hollered back," "Alright. Put your shooter in this here. (the fellow up in the tower began lowering a bucket on a rope) Take him on up to the Warden's office. I'll call and let 'em know."The officer put his gun in the bucket and the guard hoisted it up to his perch for safekeeping.

After placing Luke back in the bus, they headed on up the road past the two old boys who was still dog eyeing Luke as they passed.

About a quarter mile up the dusty road stood an old two-story house that looked to be pretty well maintained with an immaculate lawn being tended by two more men in white. The old house had a veranda styled porch upon which were two old wooden rocking chairs and a small table with a cane chair nestled up to it. There was a black Ford and a saddled horse tied to the porch handrail.

As Luke was again taken out of the bus and walked up toward the five steps leading to the veranda, the screen door to the house opened up and out walked another one of those cowboy fellas with a carbine, followed closely by an older, rather portly man in khaki pants, white dress shirt, black tie and tan work boots with one pant leg barely tucked inside. He was wearing a Panama straw hat and Luke noticed a 38 Special strapped low on his side, kinda drooping to his right side from under that big belly.

"What you got me there Chambers?" the big man asked in a brusque, smoky voice. "This here is Luther Dee Price. Got his papers right here Warden Byrton. Mr. Price here is convicted of 2nd degree murder and looks like he gonna be with you'all about twenty years or so. Got his papers right here," he repeated as he handed the manila envelope to the warden.

Big Jim took the envelope and sat down in one of the rockers. He flicked his Panama onto the seat of one of the other rockers, opened the envelope and pulled out the papers as the cowboy guy stood watching silently with the carbine resting across his arms.

"Well let's see now," Big Jim said as he looked over the commitment documents. "Let me sign this here receipt of custody for you officer so you can get on back to Pine Bluff."

Jim fumbled for a pen out of the pocket protector in his shirt pocket and signed the receipt and handed it back to the officer which he folded up and placed in his own pocket.

The guard then bent down to take the shackles off Luke's ankles, and then removed the handcuffs that Luke had been worrying with for the past forty-five minutes plus.

"Alright there Price, you take it easy on these fellas," he quipped. "'Preciate you Warden," the guard said as he tipped his hat and turned to leave. "The pleasures been all mine Chambers." Jim replied, with a hint of sarcasm.

As the bus rolled away in a cloud of dust, Luke stood silently watching as the warden continued to look over the documents. Finally, Big Jim looked up at Luke and, through squinting eyes, seemed to be kind of sizing Luke up.

Big Jim looked over at the cowboy guy and said, "Caruthers, looks like we got us a cold blooded killer here. We don't get many cold blooded killers down here do we

22

Caruthers?" he added sarcastically. "No sir, we don't," the cowboy guy replied cooly.

"Luther? you don't mind if I call you Luther do you?" The warden asked. "No sir. But most everybody calls me Luke." "Ok then Luke it is, Luke,we run a pretty tight ship here at Cummins and we don't like anybody upsettin' the apple cart if you know what I mean. Now, Caruthers here is gonna assign you to a work detail and it aint gonna be easy, but not much here is easy until you earn the *privilege* of easy. "If you follow by the rules here you gonna be alright. If you don't follow the rules, you *aint* gonna be alright." The warden put heavy emphasis on the word "aint"! "Do you understand what I'm tellin' you son?" "Yes sir I do," Luke replied. "Good, good then. So long as we understand each other there aint gonna be no problems right?" "That's right warden. There aint gonna be no problems." Luke repeated.

"Caruthers, why don't you go ahead and take ol' Luke here down to the barracks and get him suited out and settled in.

Caruthers motioned Luke down the steps and mounted the horse as Luke stood by.

"Ok boy, we gonna head back down that way, and you be sure and stay in front of me. Got it?" Caruthers ordered. "I got it," Luke replied.

They took off in the direction of the sally port at a leisurely pace at first, then Luke heard the horse and rider seemingly picking up pace and getting closer. Luke picked up his speed in order to stay ahead of Caruthers as ordered, and the sweat was beginning to pour.

After a few more steps the horse was once again breathing down on Luke and once again Luke increased his speed to a very fast walk. The horse was snorting almost in Luke's ear by now, and they moved to a gallop. Halfway to the sally port, Luke noticed that the two cowboy dudes that were there earlier had now moved on, and for some reason he was relieved about that

This was a race between man and horse, and out the corner of the man's eyes, he could see the horse was about to win. Now in a dead run, Luke felt he was about to pass out when they final made it to the sally port. Caruthers reined his horse to an abrupt stop just below the guard tower and hurriedly dismounted just as Luke was running up.

Panting, sweating and completely exhausted, Luke stopped when he finally caught up to Caruthers. Using his forearm to wipe the sweat from his eyes, he looked at Caruthers to see what was coming next.

"You're a pretty good runner Price. But I tell you one thing boy, I ever see you runnin' when I don't tell you to run, I'm gonna put one of these 30/30s right up your ass. You got that?"

"Yes sir," Luke said, "I got it." "Hold on there boy. First thing you gotta learn is, the only sir around here is the Warden his'self. From now own you refer to me as "boss," and any of these other riders you refer to as boss too!" "Yes sir boss," Luke dutifully replied.

"Jones!" Caruthers shouted to the man in the tower. Buzz this gate and let me show this fella to his new digs."He buzzed and Luke and Caruthers stepped thru.

CHAPTER FOUR

LESSONS LEARNED

As the two men passed thru the gate Luke saw a half dozen guys in white tending the grassy areas that surrounded the barracks and mess hall. Some were pushing old style rotary mowers and some were weeding with hoes and another one was watering the grass. None of them looked away from their duties.

They walked up to a building with the number "2" in a big black letter stenciled on the heavy steel door. Caruthers pulled the door open and motioned for Luke to step inside.

Luke thought it strange that Caruthers still carried the carbine, when, the tower guard had made the deputy surrender his gun up to the tower. It soon became apparent that these riders carried their guns wherever they went and didn't give 'em up to anybody; with the possible exception of the Warden himself.

Luke followed Caruthers as they stepped into a door-less room just beyond the entry door. There was an older black man sitting at a small desk smoking a hand-rolled cigarette and qawking at some sort of magazine.

"Chicken!" Caruthers said to the man in a brusque tone. "Get this man some whites and a bed roll. What size you wear

Price? Shirt, pants, shoes?" "Uh, 42 shirt, 32 pants and nine shoes," Luke answered.

The old man turned to a row of shelves lining the wall and started picking clothes and piling them onto the desk. "They's a box of brogans over there son, just pick yo' self out a good pair," the old man directed. Luke did as he was told and began fumbling through the crate to find a decent pair of work boots. Satisfied that he had found the best of the bad, Luke picked them out of the box and sat them on the floor near his feet.

"Listen up Price," Caruthers ordered. "Strip down, grab a towel over there and that jug of lice shampoo and get your ass in that shower stall and clean yourself up. After you get done, get dressed in these here whites and post your ass right here by this door and don't you move til I get back. Chicken, you get his street clothes and take 'em over to the riders' shack and tell Mosely I said get 'em washed up in case some of the boys want 'em. You got that old man?" "Yes sir boss, I sho does," the old man answered.

As soon as Caruthers left, Luke got undressed and stepped onto the shower like he was told and turned on the water. "Aint no hot in there mista'," the old man cautioned. "prob'ly gonna freeze them nuts off, but when you git in da barracks they got hot water a plenty."

"I gots to take these duds over yonder an' I be back in a jiffy. Better do what boss Caruthers say now, you don't wants no trouble," cautioned the old man. Luke nodded as the old man shuffled out of the room.

Luke turned on the faucet and rather than try to slowly get used to the cold water, he just jumped right under the flow. It took Luke's breath away for a little bit but soon it was feeling pretty damned good to him. The shampoo stunk to high hell, but he used it anyway.

When Luke finished, he stepped out and dried himself off then began to dress himself in the new/old clothes.

As Luke was lacing up the brogans, the old black man shuffled back in and Luke decided to engage him in conversation.

Hey old-timer, how long you been here?" "I's been down here since...well, let me see now, yeah, I's been down here since nineteen and thirty-nine. Yes suh, nineteen and thirty nine."

"Goddamn ol' buddy, what'd you do?" Luke asked. "Awww well, I went and took me some smokin' tobacco out of a grocery store up there in Forrest City." "How much a sentence did they give you?" "That old judge up there gave me a five-year sentence." "Five years for stealin' cigarettes? " "Well yeah, da problem is, was that sto' belonged to da judge brother-n-law." "How come you still here?" "Well suh, I has a little trouble followin' da rules. Always been that way.

Warden Byrton say I keeps my nose clean, my mouth shut and tend to business, I prob'ly be outa here nex' year." A wisp of a smile came across Chicken's weathered face.

Luke felt compassion for the old man and it probably showed in his face. "Well, I hope you do get out of here next year sir, I hope you do. Hey, tell me this, how them old boys get the job totin' them rifles?" The old man leaned in closer to Luke and in a softer voice said, "You got to be willin' an' able to do whatever the Warden say." And in an even lower whisper he said, "Don't hurt none to be an asshole neither."

Luke kinda chuckled at the old convict's remark and then he noticed the expression on the old man's face got serious... and then the lights went out.

Something hit Luke in the back of his neck like a ton of bricks!

Caruthers had slipped up behind Luke and cracked him upside his head with the butt of the carbine and Luke went to his knees involuntarily.

"I thought I told you to post your ass by that door till I got back boy?" Caruthers demanded. Luke was too shell shocked to even answer or comprehend what had just happened.

27

"Now you listen to me and you listen real good boy. When I tell you to do somethin', you do it! If I tell you to suck this old man's dick, you do it! If I tell you to eat dogshit you eat dogshit!. Do I make myself clear?" "Yeah boss." Luke replied, his ears still ringing from the blow.

"Alright then. pick that fuckin' bedroll up and follow me." Luke complied.

Still dazed, Luke followed Caruthers out into the hall where they turned left. As they walked on down the hallway Luke noticed the right side of the hall was lined with jail bars floor to ceiling and about every thirty feet or so, the rooms behind the bars was divided with cinderblock walls and in each individual room he saw about twenty-five metal beds with the bedding made up military style.

Caruthers stopped at the second room and motioned Luke inside. "Pick out an empty rack and get it made up. Chow is in about thirty minutes Price. After you eat, you can take the rest of the day to get used to the place. Tomorrow, you goin' out on a hoe squad. That's when your fun begins boy. Caruthers turned and left.

As he looked around for an empty bed, Luke realized there was one other man in the barracks laying on a rack next to an empty one. Luke decided to take the bed beside the man and headed in that direction.

CHAPTER FIVE

A FRIEND

The man on the rack was a young fellow, probably about Luke's age. He lay on the bed watching Luke with a curious eye.

"How you doing buddy?" the man asked. "Hangin' in there I guess. At least til that son-of-a-bitch hit me with that fuckin' gun. What's that dude's problem?" Luke asked incredulously. "He aint got no problem. In case you aint noticed yet, we the one with the problem." Luke didn't see the humor in the man's comment, but it was sure starting to sink in that he did have a problem for sure.

"Well buddy, what you gotta know 'bout ol' Caruthers there is that he had a bad upbringin' and he likes to take it out on us unfortunate ones. Hell, all them fuckin' riders is like that. Like they all got a spur up they asses or something'. They real particular 'bout gettin' their respect... an' what they say is what you better do!"

The man raised up and offered his hand to Luke. "Hank Short. Everybody jus' calls me Shorty." Luke put out his hand and noticed that Shorty's hand was hard as a rock. "Luke Price...and everybody just calls me Punchin' Bag." Both men had a chuckle.

"What you in for?" Shorty asked. "Second degree. But I didn't do it." Shorty looked at Luke in a way that made

Luke feel like he was being sized up. "Well, maybe you didn't but I sure as hell did. Not murder though. I held up filling station over in Texarkana and the sum-bitch pulled a gun on me. It was either have a shootout or get out! I picked get-out, but that fucker put one in my right ass cheek as I was hittin' the door. Police and ambulance got there, and as they say, the rest is history. Doin' a ten-year bit. Already got three and a half under my belt and gotta do at least seven to be eligible." "Eligible for what?" Luke asked. "Well for parole of course. In the state of Arkansas you got to do at least two-thirds of your time to be eligible for parole, which is if you committed a crime involvin' a weapon. But if you did something to hurt or kill someone, well, I guess your lawyer done explained that you gotta flatten your time 'fore you get out." Shorty kind of hung his head a little, as if he thought he was guilty of bearing bad news.

Luke knew that unless something good happened to him concerning his case he was going to do the whole twenty.

"Yeah I know. But my lawyer says he's gonna keep working on my case till he gets me out." "You have a paid lawyer, or is he a public defender?" "Couldn't afford to pay for no lawyer, he was a public defender." "I wish you luck with that, but you know who pays them PD's checks don't you? " Luke shook his head in the negative. "The fuckin' state of Arkansas! I had a public defender too! Hell Luke, if we'd a had money we prob'ly wouldn't be sittin' here today. Well, at least you might not."

Luke didn't miss the value of those words. Real justice doesn't apply to poor folks. Bias in the American judicial system had always been a fact and always would be.

"What you say we go get somethin' to eat? I'll show you around the joint and hook you up with some of the boys. Chow aint that good, but they's plenty of it." "Sounds good to me. I could eat the ass out of a horse!" "Oh, you gonna get plenty of looking at horse ass." Shorty proclaimed.

As the men left the barracks headed toward the chow hall, Luke was bemused at the fact that none of the doors were locked. This was jail after all.

"How come they don't keep us locked in?" He asked Shorty. "Well, we are locked inside the fence. You aint going out there 'cept to work, and them riders watch you like a hawk outside the fence." "What do you think they'll put me to doing?"

"Hell everybody coming in starts on the long line. Get ready for that shit man; it's a mother-fucker. 'Especially in the summer. Your ass gonna be draggin' here in the fall too! Be harvesting the cotton crop 'for too long. Right now we scabowing the cotton plants." "What the hell is scabowing? Luke asked. "That's where you take your hoe, and go down the cotton rows and chop out the weeds. You'll be goin'at a pretty good clip too! They don't stand for no bullshit out there on the line. They want that cotton brought in 'cause that's what lines the warden's pockets, and the warden don't stand for nobody dippin' in his pockets. "How come you aint workin today? Luke asked. "They's some big wig comin' down from Little Rock to talk to me today. Aint got a clue 'bout what it's about, but I got my marchin' orders from Cap'n Phillips, and he said to keep my wits about me and don't go stirrin' up no shit." Shorty leaned in a little closer to Luke and said in a softer tone, "He prob'ly wants to talk about them graves."

"Graves? What graves?" Luke asked. "Awww, I'll tell you about it in a little bit." Shorty seemed to kind of brush it off, but for sure, Luke couldn't wait to hear this one.

As the two new friends made it to the chow hall, Luke noticed that just outside the front gate, a long line of weary looking men were making their way toward the gate being led by one of the riders on horseback.

There were about forty men in the column, and each one of them was carrying a hoe across his shoulder like soldiers carry their guns. They were all dressed in the familiar white

31

clothes with straw hats except for one man in the rear pushing a two-wheeled cart that appeared to have two metal water cans with metal dippers jangling from the sides and tied to each with a small chain.

As the parade made it to the gate the rider commanded the men to stop. "Hold up right there. Drop 'em," the rider barked. The men let their hoes drop to the ground to the side of where they stood. Each one starring forward, they all looked very haggard to Luke.

"Fall out, get that grub you fuckin' dirt balls. Fifteen minutes. You know the routine. When you get done sloppin,' line up back over here at this gate. Move!" the rider shouted.

By this time Luke and Shorty had moved inside the chowhall and got in a line already occupied by about six others. Shorty picked up a metal plate and fork and started down the chow line. Luke followed suit.

The food was being served by three other inmates who were also wearing whites, but these guys also had white bandanas ties around their sweating heads.

As they progressed down the line Luke held out his tray and was given pie shaped piece of cornbread that smelled pretty damned good to Luke. Next, he was given a chunk of what looked like boiled pork and a decent helping of soup beans. Finally, Luke held out his tray and was served a big wedge of raw onion

At the end of the serving line sat a cart with plastic tumblers of semi-cool, semi-sweet tea.

Luke and Shorty took their seats at a wooden table with wooden benches on each side, that looked like it would seat about ten men.

By this time, the men from the column were filing in and sitting down after getting their food.

Luke saw that another column of marchers was making their way toward the gate from about a quarter of a mile away.

"What you doin' slacker?" one of the men said to Shorty as he sat down at their table. "Showin' this old boy the ropes

Jesse." Shorty replied. "New meat huh? Jesse inquired looking at Luke. "Yeah, he just got here today. Where'd you say you was from?" Shorty directed at Luke.

"Blytheville," Luke answered. "No shit?" Said Jesse. "Hell I'm from Jonesboro. Spent quite a bit of time over in Blytheville. What brings you down here?" "Got caught up in a murder case." Luke said. "No shit?" Jesse who apparently had a propensity for saying "no shit", inquired yet again.

"Did you do it?" "Nope. Somebody killed my best friend and a girl he was with. They found me with his car, and my knife stuck in him." Luke pondered what he had just stated. Hell, if he didn't know better, he would think he had done it too!

"Oh yeah, I heard about that. Matter of fact, that girls husband is over at Tucker. I hear tell they didn't want you two on the same unit. 'Fraid one of you might kill the other, and they'd be out a field hand." Jesse said sardonically.

"I aint got nothin' against that dude," Luke said. "Now he might think he's got somethin' against me if he thinks I killed his ol' lady, but I aint too sure his alibi was all it was cracked up to be.

"Alright all you maggots! Get your asses lined up! Let's move it!" the rider that brought the first line in to the chow hall barked. "Gotta make room for two squad. All your girlfriends gotta eat too!"

Luke and the rest of the men got up from the tables and started moving quickly to the slop can situated near the entry to the mess, where they each, in turn, dumped the contents, or what little was left of it into the barrels.

Luke and Shorty started walking back toward the barracks when a rider hollered out to Shorty.

"Short, get your ass at the back of my squad. Warden wants you up to the office. You follow us up there." "Yes sir boss!" Shorty responded with a quizzical look.

Shorty took off after the line and turned to Luke and said, "See you in a little bit man."

The riders always kept their mounts to the rear of any column they were leading so that they could watch the men closely. If anybody started lagging or getting out of line, they had a good view of who the trouble maker was and would take appropriate action. Sometime that action was overkill. The Arkansas long riders, to a man, seemed to get a kick out of bullying their charges. They had bullying down to a science as a matter of fact.

In the meantime Luke caught up to old Chicken who was going to the barracks as well."Hey old timer, you got a minute? Luke asked him. "Oh, I guess I aint got nuttin' but minutes an' hours, an' days," the old convict answered. "You know of a fella by the name of Buddy Wright that came through here recently?"

"Buddy Wright, Buddy Wright," The old man seemed to be searching his memory for the answer. "Yeah, yes sir, I sho do. They sent him over to Tucker 'bout a week ago. That boy was some bad news. Ol' boss Billings broke his arm fo' him very first thing when he got here for smart talkin' him. I told that boy jus' like I told you.

You better hold your shits when it come to them bosses. They aint got no problem fuckin' some peoples up! Naw sir, no problems what so never."

"Anyhow, he's over to the Tucker farm I believes. But I tell you what, I heard that boy say he wadn't scared of none of d'ese bosses. Said he done kil't befo' and he wadn't worried none 'bout doin' it some mo'. Yesir, that boy was a scary-un."

This bit of information stunned Luke to the core. Could it really be possible that this guy actually killed Tiny and Mindy? Luke knew he had to get to this guy or somehow get evidence to prove that either Buddy Wright killed the two, or, that he himself had not.

Back in the barracks, Luke lay on his rack and thought about the situation.

The more he thought about it, the more he was convinced that Buddy did have something to do with the murders. Hell, somebody beside Luke was guilty, of that he was sure. But, stuck here in this hell hole, with that dude fifty miles away at Tucker, how the hell was he gonna get anything done.

After thinking about it, he decided his best chance was to get in touch with his lawyer and see if he could do something, and the only way he had to get in touch with Ronnie was to write him a letter.

Let him know what he was thinking and see if Ronnie thought it was worth looking into. Luke himself sure as hell thought it was.

Fortunately, in most prison systems, legal mail between an inmate and his attorney is privileged information, and cannot be read by prison officials, so Luke decided to send Ronnie a letter.

Dear Ronnie,   Oct. 2, 1987

   Just wanted to let you know
that I made it down here and
it's as bad as I had heard.
   Got hit in the head by a rifle
butt first thing.
   Already met a couple of guys
here and I think I will be able
to get along ok.

   What I really want to mention
to you is about Mindy's husband,
Buddy Wright.
   Ronnie, I think there is a good
possibility that Buddy killed Tiny
and Mindy.
   He's already bragged around that
he has killed someone.
   Buddy is at Tucker.
   I would thank you to look into
this for me.

               Sincerely,
               Luke Prince

P.S,
   Let me know.

At around five o: clock that afternoon, the hoe squads started coming in from the fields, and at least for today, their work was over and they were free to sit back in the barracks and re-coup their energy and smoke cigarettes and put the day behind them.

Luke noticed that Shorty had not made it back from the warden's office yet and was worried if something had happened. Just as the thought crossed his mind, Shorty walked through the door looking a little worse for the wear. Luke could see even from a distance that Shorty had split lip and was bruised around his left eye.

"What the hell happened to you man?" "Seems like the warden wanted to make sure my story was gonna be to his liking before I talked to that State man, so he had one of the bosses make sure I got my story straight. Started telling the warden what I thought I knew about us finding some buried bodies down by the levy. All I told him was that me and the rest of the squad was takin' a shade break down there a couple months back, you know, just sittin' there bullshittin' an' all when I was kinda scrapin' at the dirt with my boot and it sounded kinda hollow. So when the the boss was takin' a piss, me and one of the boys started digging a little deeper, and sure as hell, they was a wooden box buried there.

It was kinda rotten and all and it was pretty easy to pry one of the boards loose and inside that box they was a set of skeleton eyes staring out at me. Goddamn Luke, that gave me the willies for sure! We got to looking around us and we could see four or five, kinda like depressions in the ground. Looked like to us there was a bunch of bodies buried around there,"

"So we called the boss over and he looked at it and says for us to get our asses back to work and not worry 'bout old cemetery bullshit! Luke, I guarantee you that weren't no goddamn old cemetery. Somebody had put the bodies there within the past few years; and we got to thinking about it,but a couple inmates from here came up missin' just since I been here.

Nobody knew whether they was paroled or escaped. They jus' up an disappeared, and I been hearin' stories that it's happened more than once."

"So after the boss man got me straightened out, the state man shows up and I go tell him what the warden wanted me to." What did he want you to tell 'em? "That it was just an old cemetery, been there for years. He wanted to know if I could take him to the place and I told him I didn't remember exactly where it was. I don't think that ol' state boy believed me though, I could just kinda see it in his eyes. I gotta tell you Luke, I'm a little bit afraid that state boys' going to come back and start diggin' around out there and the warden is gonna come down hard on my ass!"

What kind of hell had Luke got himself into with this place? The whole goddamned state knew this was a very bad place to be, but could these people really just kill inmates and get away with it?

Luke didn't even want to think about the ramifications of the answer, but he knew that while he was here, he was gonna do his best to tow-the-line and not get himself caught in the sights of these fucking barbarians.

Luke kept pondering the things he'd heard and seen on this first day in the joint. It was all at once very interesting and extremely un-nerving.

As the inmates lounged around the barracks making small talk and engaging in occasional horseplay and smoking home rolled smokes, Luke asked Shorty about the old man Chicken.

"Why you reckon they call that fella Chicken? he asked. "Aw hell, I know why he got that name. His real name is Porter Ray, but way back when he got here, his job was workin' the pig farm and chicken coops. For Warden Byrton's entertainment, he would go down to the coops on killin' day and watch old Chicken kill them birds that wasn't producing eggs no more. When the old man got to the last bird, the warden would have him cut the chickens head off, and then would make him turn that chicken's body up and drink its blood right out of its cutoff neck. Makes me wanna puke just thinkin' 'bout it!" Luke was dumbfounded.

Shorty started talking to Luke about what working the hoe squad would be like and what was expected of him. Tomorrow would be Luke's first day on the line and he was feeling a little apprehensive. Luke wasn't afraid of work. Hell, he had been working since he was a little boy, the paper routes, mowing lawns, washing cars; but when he was about eighteen, he landed a job with a house framing crew. After three years of learning the trade, he decided it was time to set out on his own and start his own crew. He was fairly successful virtually from the start and actually became a master carpenter.

To get rid of the associated tension of hard days and lonely nights, Luke would occasionally go to bars and bowling alleys. He met his first love at the bowling alley in Blytheville.

CHAPTER SIX

LIVIN' n LOVIN'

Time and time again, Luke's mother had told him that a good life would be dictated by the ones we chose to live with. Sara and Thomas Price had lived a good life, not an opulent or easy life, but a good one, nurtured by love and respect for each other and the children they raised.

In nineteen-forty-one, the good Lord had blessed Sara and Tom with a little girl.

Pam was the apple of her daddy's eye and she brought a nice sparkle to those eyes when Tom would get home from work at the Nibco Foundry, where Tom had worked his way to lead maintenance man after joining the company in nineteen-forty.

Forty to fifty hours a week was the norm for Tom, and the overtime at $5. an hour in the 1950's helped a lot to keep the bills paid and food on the table, plus the other little things that made life in the Mississippi river town, if not enjoyable, at least bearable.

They had even managed to make a down payment on that little house on South Franklin Street.

Soon after they bought that house, a little boy made his way into the world.

Luther Dee Price was born on July 3, 1942 at 11:40 pm. If he'd held out another twenty minutes, he would have been a firecracker baby. Tom always thought his boy was a firecracker anyway.

Little Pam had a hard time pronouncing her baby brothers name and it came out sounding like "Luker Tee", so, it just morphed into "Luke" as a matter of course.

A tow headed dirty blond; you could find Luke all over the town of twenty-five thousand if you could find him at all. Hunting crawdads in the ditches or swimming in the deep curb gutter down by the YMCA after a big rain was what Luke liked. He had the usual friends and they always seemed to be into some kind of boy mischief. Nothing serious mind you, just the stuff little boys like to do.

One tme Luke and his best friend Tiny Joe, found an old washtub and, that, to them, was the perfect sailing vessel.

They took that old tub, which was just about big enough for a normal sized nine-year-old boy to ride in, down to a run-off ditch out on North Ruddle Road, with intentions of taking turns sailing that yacht down the raging rapids of that ditch all the way to China.

Luke never made it to China in that old washtub, but he did do a fine job of navigating it all the way down to old Mr. Cockerel's stock crossing about a mile away; where he forgot to duck as the tub went under the low lying pipe bridge, rewarding Luke with a decent little gash to the top of his noggin'.

The old tub washed on down the stream never to be seen again, but Luke managed to get hold of a length of chain dangling from the bridge, and hung on until Tiny got there and fished him out of the ditch; bloody head and all.

And there was the time when Luke, Tiny and a couple of other friends were playing at the old abandoned cotton gin at the north end of Franklin Road,

That old gin was the ultimate fort for pre-teen boys. High lofts, old equipment, hidden passageways ropes to swing from and Luke's favorite was the old rusty circa WW2 Willis Jeep. That thing was Luke's command car from which he led many an attack against the advancing hordes. Although it hadn't ran in more than twenty years, it ran good just good enough to suit Luke's imagination.

Anyway, on this particular day, the boys were having their usual game of war, hiding and hunting, when Luke stepped from a doorway and looked up toward the upper level. One of the other boys, (who it was Luke could not recall) accidentally kicked a chunk of oak planking that must have been two or three feet long and weighed at least five pounds, off the side of the thirty-foot level of the gins loft. That hunk of oak caught Luke right smack dab on the top of his head not too far from the scar left by the pipe bridge, but fortunately it was only a glancing blow.

Luke wasn't going to pass up an opportunity to lend a little drama to the action, so he promptly went to the ground in a heap and feigned unconsciousness. (although it did smart a bit)

The other boys came running from all directions to converge on the body of their fallen comrade, or sworn enemy, whichever the case may have been, to give lifesaving relief.

"Luke!, Luke!, are you ok?" Tiny implored. Luke just lay there playing it off with one eye half open, and purposefully letting a little drool run down the side of his cheek for effect.

"Uhhhh," Luke moaned. "Ohhh!" as he continued to over-act.

"Come on fellas, we gotta get him home," Tiny ordered. Everyone grabbed an arm or a leg and started hauling Luke's limp body in the direction of Luke's house at the other end of Franklin Road.

Halfway home, Luke couldn't help but feel good about the scam he was perpetrating on his friends and began to giggle and laugh.

The boys, finally realizing that they had been duped, unceremoniously dumped Luke on the ground in a heap. At that point they giggled and laughed as a group. However, by this time a quite impressive rooster egg of a lump had begun growing on Luke's head.

The winter of 1944 brought another baby girl to the Price family.

Betty Ruth came into the world on December 7th; exactly three years after the Japanese had bombed Pearl Harbor, and just a few months before the end of WW2.

Tom had been called up for the draft during the war, but never had to go due to a 4F classification because of a back injury he had suffered in 1939 at the foundry.

That 4F didn't disqualify him from making babies however.

The birth of Betty was pretty stressful for mother and child. Betty was what they called a "breech" baby. Basically, the way Luke understood it, she was born upside down, feet first, and the umbilical had gotten around the babies neck and she was deprived of her mother's lifesaving blood which provided that necessary oxygen. In the doctor's panic, he held off the delivery for several minutes while waiting on another doctor to show up and assist with the delivery. This nearly cost Betty her life, and Sara was stressed as well.

The little girl was finally delivered but it was touch and go for several days as she lay in the intensive care unit for newborns.

In spite of a dubious beginning, Betty grew up to be a relatively healthy child, but she was somewhat frail, and on to[of that was a bit of a wallflower for most of her life; at least until she met that jet jock from the air force base... then she seemed to, well... blossom!

On one of those sweltering, humid, mosquito infested delta nights that you need to experience to "appreciate", Luke sat on the front porch of his little house. It was August 1966 when the phone rang inside the house.

Trying to decide on whether or not to put the cold Coors down or answer the phone, Luke hum hawed for a moment then decided he could keep the Coors *and* answer the phone.

"Hello." "Hey old buddy, why don't you get your ass down here? I got somebody I think you ought to meet." It was Tiny trying to set Luke up with another blind date. "Aw, I don't know T. Thought I'd just sit around and take it easy this weekend. Where you at anyway?" "Down at the bowling alley. Sherry's cousin came in and she wants to meet you brother man." "This aint no bullshit neither man. This gal is a real sweetie-pie." "Yeah, I know all about your idea of sweet, hoss." Luke responded with a bit of good-natured sarcasm.

"Naw. This time I'm for real. You gonna be missin' out like a loser if you don't get down here.

Luke parked his truck near the entrance to the bowling alley and walked inside.

Tiny Joe was sitting in the café with two girls. One was Sherry Perry. Luke figured Sherry's parents had a little bit of a weird sense of humor by naming her like that, but Sherry was a pretty decent girl. And she seemed to be head over heels for Tiny.

Next to Sherry sat a girl who looked like a heaven sent angel. Tiny didn't lie about this one.

"Whaz up budreau?" Tiny asked as Luke sauntered up to the table. Luke shrugged shyly. "This here's Leslie. She's Sherry's cousin like I told you. Leslie, this here's Luther Dee Price. We just call him Luke 'cause just plain ol'asshole don't go over very good in some circles." They all laughed at Tiny's attempt at humor.

Luke held out his hand. "Pleased to meet you ma'am," Luke offered. "Same here Luke. Sherry has told me a lot about you. She says you are a pretty good carpenter." "He sure is

44

honey!" chimed in Sherry. "He built my daddy a work shop out behind the house, and daddy won't leave that place for nothing!" "Yeah, that's what I love to do." Luke offered.

"That aint *all* you love to do!" Tiny chimed in. Luke was a bit embarrassed by Tiny's remarks, but as usual he took it in stride, giving back that sheepish grin.

"Want somethin' to eat ol' buddy? Tiny asked. "Nah, I had a bite a little while ago. I will take one of those beers though.

Tiny motioned the waitress over and ordered Luke a Coors.

"So, where are you from Leslie?" Luke asked. "I'm actually from Lexington, Kentucky. But I just moved here from St. Louis. I thought I would give it a try down here. See what happens."

"What do you do?" Luke asked. "I'm a hairdresser." She replied. "I already have a job lined up at Cut N Curl down in Osceola." "You gonna live in Osceola? That's twenty miles down 61 you know?" "I'm going to stay with Sherry until I get a better handle on what I want to do, but... now I'm thinking I kind of like it right here." She answered shyly, grinned and turned her head a bit. Luke liked that.

Over the next several months, Luke and Leslie became quite the item. They were seen all over the place. Restaurants, the drive-in theater, Walker Park in Blytheville and of course the skating rink.

Luke had never been too serious about any girl really, but this girl did something to him that generally knocked his socks off... literally!

The couple enjoyed spending time at Luke's place just kicking back and enjoying each other's company. They had even been talk about moving in together but that was really just talk for the time being.

It seems that Leslie had a son back in St. Louis, five years old, who was being looked after by Leslie's parents until she was able to give him a decent life herself.

Leslie had told Luke that the break-up from the boy's father was less than amicable; apparently the guy had been a drunk and somewhat abusive to her and the kid, and she had decided to get away from him and start fresh.

Luke couldn't figure out why someone would be mean to a girl like Leslie, but he knew there were all kinds of people in the world and everyone has to pick and choose who they associated themselves with. Luke was all too happy that Leslie had chosen him to be with during this time in their lives. In fact, between his work and Leslie, he was about the happiest man in the world.

In the spring of '65, bad news came to the Price family. Sara had been feeling poorly for some time now, and the recent death of Tom had made life seem more like a chore than anything else.

Tom had came down with a severe cold the previous winter, and it had turned into pneumonia in just a few days. The doctors did all they could of course, but antibiotics had not done the trick and Tom passed a few days before his 42nd birthday. Much too young for a guy like Tom who had always been so full of life, and who had been the rock of the family.

Now, less than a year later, Betty found her mom crumpled on the floor between the bed and dresser in her bedroom.

It was a beautiful Sunday morning. Just the kind of day where you would find Sara on the porch shelling peas, or hanging laundry on the line.

But on this day, she'd had a stroke. A bleeding vessel in her brain, that didn't care about anything serene or beautiful. All it was designed to do was kill or maim; and in this instance it killed a families' spirit.

By the time Luke arrived at the hospital, Sara was in a comatose state, not knowing anyone or anything.

It absolutely crushed Luke and the girls when the doctor told them there was no hope for recovery. It was just a matter of time. Sara could linger for days, months or years.

As it turned out, it was only days. Sara passed from the world the following Thursday.

On the next Saturday morning, Sara Price was laid to rest at the Dogwood Cemetery just on the outskirts of Blytheville. She was next to Tom again.

Luke and the girls had decided to put the house on Franklin up for sale. It was a sad thing to let go of that house, but they each had their own lives now.

Pam was soon to be on her way to Germany with her husband, and Betty was pretty heavily involved with her knew beau. There would most likely be a new marriage sometime in the near future. Until the house sold, Betty and Luke would stay there; at least until Luke finished building his little cottage out near Bell Fountain Ditch.

Bell Fountain Ditch wasn't really a ditch at all, and it wasn't even "Bell Fountain". That was actually a bastardization of the French "Belle Fontaine". It was one of many irrigation canals built in the middle 30's by President Roosevelts WPA to provide irrigation and flood control to the farmlands in the Delta.

Luke had managed to purchase five acres of land just the previous year, that backed up to the canal with the intentions of building a little place he could claim as his own. It would be finished in a couple of months.

By the middle of summer 1967, Leslie had made a couple of trips back up to St. Louis to visit her boy and her mother. Luke had not met the little boy yet, and it seemed as if he may not get the opportunity.

Every time Leslie returned from St. Louis, she seemed a little distant...not quite as affectionate. Luke couldn't explain it or understand it, but he knew there was change ahead; and he didn't like the feeling.

Luke and Leslie got together one night in July, and she finally told him what had been going on.

The boy's father had been trying to get Leslie to come back to St. Louis to try for reconciliation. She said she had been putting him off, trying to get her mind right and all, but had not made her decision yet.

This hit Luke like a ton of bricks. It was becoming obvious to him that she apparently still had feelings for the guy or, hell, she wouldn't even be considering it!

"I don't know what to say," Luke proclaimed solemnly. "I thought we had a good thing here. Was I wrong?" "We do have a good thing Luke. I care for you greatly. I...I just want to do what's best for my son; *me* and my son!"

"Do you love him Leslie?" "No...oh I don't think so Luke, I'm so confused. There was some bad things that went on between him and me and I just need some time to work this out. I'm so happy having you in my life, but I miss my little boy so much, and I can't bring myself to take him away from my mother...or his daddy. I need you to help me with this Luke." "You mean you want me to say its ok?"

"If you still care for this guy Leslie, I'm not so sure I want to compete with that. All I can tell you is, that I love you and want to get to know and love your son too!"

Luke didn't sleep well that night, or for many nights thereafter for that matter.

He had dreams of himself, Leslie and her son living a nice little un-complicated life out on Bell Fountain.

CHAPTER SEVEN

CONFLUENCE OF EVIL

Luke's first day on the hoe squad proved to be as bad as he had imagined and more.

The day started at 5:am, with an electric buzzer blasting thru Luke's ears followed by one of the riders walking down the hall rubbing a metal food tray against the bars.

"Rise and shine you useless fuckers! Time to give another day to the State! Move it goddamn it!" the rider shouted.

All the men in the barracks jumped to and started getting dressed. After about ten or twelve minutes everyone had gotten dressed and moved through the lines to the toilets to shit, piss and brush their teeth… assuming they had any teeth.

The men in two barracks made their way to the chow haul to fill up on strong black coffee, grits, scrambled eggs and biscuits.

The powers that be knew that in order to get the work done on the farms, the rankmen had to be well fed. Although the quality may not have been that great, there was plenty of it and it was for the most part wholesome. Even the occasional weevil or grub added protein to the diet.

After following the other rank men's lead, Luke fell in Line next to Shorty.

"Where's your hat man?" Shorty asked Luke. Luke gritted his teeth and swore under his breath, "Shit!, left it in my box!" Shorty reached into his back Pocket and took out a faded bandana and handed it to Luke. "Here, take this and tie it around your head. You gonna need it brother."

The hoe squad started its one-mile march to the field they would be working that day, with the rider situated on his horse at the back of the line.

The sun had started to show its face in the east, and Luke was thinking this was actually a beautiful fall morning. He would soon find out that beautiful fall mornings on the unit often turned in to hell on earth.

The only sound to be heard was the shuffling of feet through dust, the rustling of hoes laid across shoulders and the occasional horse snort and whinny.

After a twenty minute march, the group made it to the appointed field. Today they would be scabowing weeds around the cotton plants.

Luke had not done too much gardening in his life, didn't have a green thump at all, but he had cut quite a bit of grass in his day and wasn't afraid of getting in there and getting a job done.

Little did Luke realize...this was a different kind of work.

"Awright you buzzards. Get them hoes down and get to it! Spread out and catch a row. Move it!" Caruthers barked.

There were thirty men on this crew, and each took a row and started heading toward the east.

Scraping and chopping at the dry ground as they went, Luke soon noticed that the other men were moving slightly ahead of him on their rows and he made a concerted effort to catch up.

Luke noticed out the corner of his eye that the rider was moving up closer to him. He kept his head down as Caruthers shouted orders.

"Price! You pussy son-of-a-bitch! What you think this is? You think you gonna lag your sorry ass behind everybody else?" "No sir boss. Just trying to get 'em all." "You need to get 'em all a damned sight faster boy!" Caruthers demanded. Luke put his head down a little farther and sped up his progress.

After an hour had gone past, the line made it to the far end of the field, and in a coordinated move, they all danced around so that each man could line up on fresh rows and start the process all over again in the opposite direction.

By this time, Luke could feel a burning in his hands and knew that blisters were forming. He had noticed earlier that a few of the men had gloves on, and right now Luke would kill for a pair of those gloves…another hard lesson…never go to the field without gloves or a hat.

After another hour, they had come to the end of another row and all total so far, they had hoed sixty rows of low cotton.

Luke amused to himself how efficient this process was, considering the fact that it was all done with manpower; actually slave-power.

"Awright boys, get you some water and catch the dirt. "Caruthers ordered. "You all got ten minutes. Smoke 'em if you got 'em"

Then, Caruthers took a long draw off the canteen he had strapped to his horse's saddle and took a real cigarette out of his pocket and lit it up. Long line riders didn't *have* to roll their own.

After the men had dropped to their collective asses, some of them took out tobacco pouches and started rolling cigarettes which they then lit with Zippo lighters or matches, whatever the case may be.

Shorty came over and sat down next to Luke as the mid-morning sun began to beat down on the weary men.

"Well... what ya think ol' buddy?" Shorty asked. "This is some pretty tough, backbreaking shit. " Luke replied. "I'll be damned lucky if I can straighten my ass out by mornin.'" "Hell, you'll get used to it sooner or later homeboy. At the very least you gonna get you a good tan out of the deal."

"On your feet!" Caruthers barked. The men once again took up their implements and started a new set of rows/

By eleven thirty, they had finished 120 rows and it was time to head in for some lunch. Luke was starving, but didn't look forward to the march back to "civilization".

"How come they make us walk all the way out here?" Luke asked Shorty. "Hell, they don't make us walk to all the fields, jus' the ones that is about a mile or less. Guess they figure it's better for us to use our energy than to waste diesel fuel firing up them tractors an' trailers.

Back at the chow hall, the men sat down to a wedge of cornbread, turnip greens, boiled chicken and that wonderful semi-sweet cold tea.

Lunch came and went way too fast in Luke's mind. It wasn't long until Caruthers was yelping again

"I'm beginning to hate that prick!" Luke said to Shorty. "Don't worry 'bout it none...he hates you too!" Shorty replied with a half-hearted grin.

That evening, at around 6:15, the men had made it back to the barracks. Luke was as tired as he had ever been in his entire life. Dog-assed tired was a pretty good description of the way he felt.

After collapsing across his bunk, Luke lay there wondering if he could possibly get up and make it into the shower...he didn't think so.

The rest of the men seemed to be no worse for the wear really, they were tired to be sure, like anyone who had put in a good days work, but Luke was bone weary. He was actually in pain.

After Luke had laid there for a while, his eyes started drooping, and before long he had passed out. Sleep felt really, really good.

"You sum'bitch, I told you to leave my shit alone! Didn't I tell you next time you wanted somethin' of mine to ask fer it?" "I aint been in your stuff man. This here deodorant is mine. Traded it off of Jenkins over there. Aint that right Jenkins?"

Two of the inmates had started arguing and this woke Luke out of his slumber.

Jenkins never said a word.

"I'm gonna whip your ass hoss. You don't jus' take my shit without askin'" "Well bring your ass on over here you bad mother-fucker. Git you some of this."

The man, who had been stolen from, Holland, lunged at the accused thief and they both fell in a heap to the concrete floor. After rolling around for a couple of minutes, neither seemed to be getting the upper hand. Then it got quiet all of a sudden, Warden Byrton and Caruthers casually strolled in to the cell block and headed in the direction of the two scufflers.

"What in hell on God's green earth you two scoundrels think you doing here?" The warden boomed. "Porter here done stole my deodorant warden and I aimed to get it back." Porter, is that right, you steal from this man? ""No sir warden. I got this from Jenkins."

Byrton turned toward Jenkins who was standing about four racks away.

"How 'bout it boy, did this here feller get that deodorant from you?" "Jenkins hesitated a moment. "No sir, he didn't get it from me, never seen it before now."

53

Porter stood there for a moment in dis-belief. "Jenkins, what you gonna go and lie for? You know I traded you a pouch of Bugle for that deodorant!" Jenkins did not reply, he just looked at the floor.

Big Jim looked for a while at Porter, then he looked at Jenkins.

"One of you cocksuckers is tellin' a lie." He hesitated...since I don't know which one it is, I'm gonna whip both your asses! Caruthers, get up to the house and fetch my strap!

By the time Caruthers returned with 'Ol Blister, Big Jim had the two men strip themselves buck assed naked and lined up out in the hallway.

"Warden, please don't do this." Porter pleaded. "Shut your goddamned mouth boy! You sons-a-bitches think you can come into my place and lie and steal and cheat, you got another shittin' thing coming. I'm gonna teach you all a lesson you aint likely soon to forget!"

"Porter, you first. Get down on your hands and knees boy and get that ass up in the air. Caruthers... if this sum-bitch moves an inch you shoot his rotten ass!" "Yes sir warden." Caruthers replied. Porter, with big tears in his eyes, did as he was told.

Luke and the other inmates were still in the barracks, but could still hear pretty well what was taking place out in the hall because it was deathly. quiet in the barracks.

What they heard in the hall shot fear and absolute loathing into their hearts.

As Big Jim brought the strap down on Porters naked flesh, they heard the old fat man grunt. Then they heard the swoosh of the leather strap streaking through the air on its way to the target, then they heard the sound of the strap popping against the inmate's buttocks, and then they heard Porter cry out in an un-earthly scream. It was the sound an animal would make when caught in a powerful trap.

And they heard these sounds five times for each of the punished men.

When it was over, Big Jim stuck his piggish face into the barracks door and ordered some of the men to come out and help Porter and Jenkins back to their racks.

It seems Jim Byrton had decided that Jenkins had stolen the deodorant from Holland, and then he traded it to Porter for smokes. In the warden's mind, both were guilty; Jenkins for stealing, and Porter for having stolen property.

Justice served Jim Byrton style.

The men's buttocks were covered in angry red welts with traces of blood beginning to seep. They lay down on their respective bunks, still whimpering like children.

The atmosphere in the barracks was now somber and subdued. It was very difficult seeing grown men broke down into their basic elements.

Absolute fear and loathing for that beast of a man was thick in the air this night at the Cummins Unit of the Arkansas Department of Corrections.

The next few weeks went by mostly uneventfully, and Luke was happy for that. Late fall was at hand at the end of November, and Luke had adjusted to the place as well as one can.

The cotton crop was now coming in. Where there was not enough mechanical cotton pickers available, the job was left to hand picking.

This was accomplished much like the chopping except the men were dragging nine-foot cotton sacks behind them down the rows and pulling the bolls from the plants and placing the cotton in the sacks behind them.

On average, it would take a trip down one and a half to two rows to get the sack full at which time the picker would haul the heavy sack to a scale that had been set up at the end of the turn row.

Each time the sack was weighed, it would generally come in at around one hundred fifty pounds. Every picker was expected to pick at least five hundred pounds per day. Anything less and there could be repercussions from the bosses.

By now, Luke's back had become somewhat accustomed to the drudgery and had actually gotten in pretty good shape, with a decent tan to boot. When the crew got back to the barracks on this day, Luke found a piece of mail laying on his rack.

Ronald Ball Law Firm
1344 West Main Street
Blytheville, Arkansas 72501
November 22,1967

Mr. Luther D. Price:

Hello Luke, I know it's been quite some time since you heard from me, but I have been pretty busy working on your case.

I think I have some good news for you however.

I've spent a good deal of time checking up on this fellow Buddy Wright.

It seems Buddy's alibi was not worth the time he took to say it. I talked to the captain of the boat and his recollection of the facts is that Buddy was <u>not </u>on the boat that night

Buddy's cousin, who lied for Buddy, was on the boat, but not Buddy. The captain has time cards to verify it.

I was also able to talk to a gentleman who worked at Scotties Truck stop out by the interstate, and he recalled seeing our friend Mr. Wright walking into the restroom at the back of the station at 2:am on the morning of the murders. He also said it looked like Buddy had a lot of blood on his shirt sleeves.

Now Luke, I have a meeting with the prosecutor in about a week. He is on vacation in Jamaica or the Bahamas, and his deputy is holding the fort down till Mr. Port returns.

I need to wait and talk to Port directly. I'm going to see if he will agree to a new trial based on what I've found.

Keep your chin up pal, and I'll let you know something when I know something.

Your Friend, Ronnie Ball

This was the best news Luke could have hoped for. He had had a feeling for a long time that Buddy Wright had committed the murders, and had taken his friend from him.

On December 1st, which was a Sunday, Luke and Shorty were sitting out on the yard, leaned up against the barracks wall near the chow hall. They were just chewing the fat and Luke had told Shorty about the letter from Ronnie.

"By God that is good news homeboy. I'm glad to hear that for you. I sure am." "I don't want to get my hopes up Shorty, but this thing may be coming to an end for me soon. Hell, I'm as excited as a fly on a turd." Both men laughed out loud.

As they were sitting there, the two men noticed that Caruthers had walked up close to where they sat.

"Short!" he barked. You got a phone call waitin' on you boy up at the warden's house."

Shorty and Luke looked at each other in puzzlement. No inmates got phone calls here, especially at the warden's house!

"What you mean boss? Shorty asked with a certain amount of nervousness in his voice. "You heard me goddamn it! Hurry your ass up now! He's waitin' on you."

Shorty got to his feet and followed Caruthers up toward the house. Shorty walked through the door to the warden's house with Caruthers and his carbine close on his heels. The old fat man was sitting on a divan on the office area puffing on a big old Cuban cigar.

"Inmate Short?" Yes sir boss?" "I am very, very disappointed in you son." The fat man said as he crossed his hands at his ample lap I found out today from a very dear friend of mine up in Little Rock, that you been secretly corresponding with one of them goddamned troublemakers up there." Big Jim's voice was slow and measured. "Is that true son?" "Why, no sir warden. I aint got no call to be talkin' with any of them folks. Hell warden, I got nothin' they'd be interested in hearing. I Swear to you sir.."

Shorty well remembered his last visit to the warden's house, and he didn't want any repeats of that shit.

"What do you think about this Caruthers?" The warden asked. "I figure he's full of shit as a Christmas turkey warden." Caruthers replied.

Big Jim took a moment looking at the ashes from his cigar as he rolled them around in a big glass ashtray.

"Yep, I'm kinda feelin' that way too Caruthers. I think we need to get this sack of shit to start actin' right."

He nodded his head, and quick as lightning, Caruthers slammed the rifle butt against the side of Shorty's head, and then Shorty's lights went out.

When Shorty came to a few minutes later, he found himself strapped to a wooden table somewhere in the bowels of the old house. He looked to the left and saw Big Jim standing there with his hands behind his back staring at him like he was admiring a shiny new car.

To the right, he noticed that Caruthers was rummaging around the upper shelf of a closet that was in the corner of the room.

The rider took down a wooden box approximately a foot square, then he turned and placed it between Shorty's legs that had been strapped to the table spread-eagle fasion. Shorty also realized his hands were tied securely to the legs of the table he was laying on. He was also aware that his pants were pulled down to his ankles, and his shoes and socks were not on his feet.

Caruthers took the lid off the box and set it aside. Inside the box was a generator from an old timey crank phone. There were also two red sheathed copper wires coiled up on the device.

"This here's that telephone call I told you about." Caruthers proudly announced. "Now, the only question is…is this gonna be a local call, or a long distance call boy? It's gonna be up to you."

"Look here boss, y'all aint gotta do this! I'm tellin' you I aint said nothing to nobody!" Shorty's voice began to sound more stressed as he begged.

"Well, we fixin' to find that out, aint we?" Big Jim proclaimed, as Caruthers took one of the wire leads and tied it around the left big toe on Shorty's foot. For the other one, he put on a pair of surgical gloves and non-too-gently tied it around Shorty's flaccid penis.

"Awright boy, here's your chance to tell us what we want to hear." Tears now started to stream from the young man's eyes.

"I don't know what you want boss. I aint done nothin', I swear on my daddy's grave!"

Big Jim made a tisk-tisk sound as he swiveled his head back and forth, then nodded to Caruthers.

Caruthers grasped the base of the device and gave the crank a couple of energetic turns and the current surged into Shorty's body. Shorty convulsed and screamed loud, and this caused Big Jim to take the handkerchief from his back pocket and stuff t into Shorty's wide open mouth.

The fat man leaned down real close to the inmate's face... close enough that he could see the pores on the man's skin and the sweat pouring out of those pores.

The convulsions showing on the tortured man's face seemed to please Big Jim greatly.

"You got somethin' you want to tell me son?"he asked. Shorty nodded yes, snorting snot and phlegm. Jim took his handkerchief from Shorty's mouth and listened intently. "I...I aint done nothin' boss. Please no more!"

Jim nodded at Caruthers once again, and once again he turned the crank, this time he made five turns of the handle.

Shorty's back arched all the way off the table as the current was applied, and this time Shorty's bladder failed him and he started squirting piss straight up in the air in spasms.

By this time, Byrton had re-lit his stogy and was puffing furiously as the urine squirted from the mans body.

Shorty seemed to be unconscious by this time, so Byrton had Caruthers get a pitcher of water and pour it on the comatose inmate.

As the cold water hit him Shorty gasped and tried to raise up but the ropes held him firmly. The veins in Shorty's neck were bulging and he was gasping for air.

"Well, how 'bout it son? You like this shit?" Jim's voice began to boom now. Shorty shook his head from side to side. "Well you goddamned well better start talkin' to me son or you gonna have you a phone bill you can't pay! You follow me you dumb sonsabitch?"

Shorty had gotten to the point where he couldn't reply even if he'd had anything to say.

"Crank it some more!" Jim ordered Caruthers. Caruthers readily complied and the juice flowed. Shorty convulsed again, but this time there were no more screams, only gurgling sounds from the man's throat and the spasms from his entire body.

Big Jim *thought* that he had the squealer, but in this case he was dead *wrong*.

The real talker was one Captain R.D. Phillips. Captain Phillips had been Jim's right hand man for over a dozen years and was well trusted by Byrton; but what Byrton didn't know was, that back in October, when that state man had been down there to talk to Shorty, he had also been approached by the Captain.

It seems the good Captain had seen the writing on the wall about this place, and he figured the writing was telling him to cut his losses while he could.

Phillips knew all about the slave labor... about how Jim had sent state inmates to work on projects for Jim's cronies. For which Jim had been paid a lot of money over the years, and he knew about the tortures and whippings.

Phillips also knew about the murders of inmates by the long line riders <u>and</u> the warden, and had even been involved in a lot of these activities himself!

Yeah, Captain Phillips knew all about that stuff, and Captain Phillips wasn't planning on getting locked up either, so Captain Phillips decided he was gonna spill the beans on the whole illicit goddamned operation.

CHAPTER EIGHT

RETRIBUTION

Luke woke up the next morning and immediately noticed that Shorty was not in his rack. He started asking around to the other guys, and no one had seen Shorty; at least not since last evening.

Before he had to get to the chow hall for breakfast, Luke walked over to the supply room to ask Chicken if he knew anything.

"Mornin' Chicken." "Hey there Luke. Aint you gonna get you some of that good breakfast this morning?" "Yes sir… but first I wanted to ask you if you've seen or heard from Shorty today?" "Naw sir, 'least not since you two was out front yesterday. Why? He aint come back?" "No, nobody's seen him.

He went up to the warden's house last night with Caruthers. Caruthers said he had a phone call. What do make of that?"

"Aww Lawd! That aint no good at all. Don't you know what that means? When they says you gots a phone call, they's gonna hook you up to that old telephone and they gonna dial yo' number awright, they gonna ring it real good!"

"I gots me one of them phone calls a few years back, an' I tell you one thang…I don't wants no mo' ! Naw sir!" The old man began to ring his hands and pace back and forth.

This was very disturbing for Luke to hear and see.

"Can it kill a man, Chicken?" "I reckons it could. Wished they'd kill't me while it was going on I tells you!"

The old man continued, "Last night, I was sittin' out front havin' me a smoke when a ambu-lance came in and headed up yonder t'wards the warden's house. A few minutes later, I seen that same ol' ambu-lance headin' back out again. Wadn't going real fast nor nuthin' and didn't have no sirens on neither."

As he spoke all the men in the barracks were heading out towards the chow hall.

"Alright Chicken, I appreciate that ol' buddy." Luke said. "Aint nuttin' to it. I sho' does hope that boy is ok… I sho' does." "Me too Chicken; me to!"

Luke made it through the day as best he could. He had already lost one good friend because of some psycho son-of-a-bitch, and he didn't want to lose another.

Back at the barracks at the end of the day, Luke was heading into the dorm when Chicken stuck his head out of his cubby-hole and motioned for Luke to come inside.

"Boss Billings was in here this mornin' and I heard him and Cap'n Phillips out in the hallway talkin'. The boss was tellin' the Cap'n that they done took Shorty up to the hospital in Pine Bluff last night. He say he was sho' 'nuff messed up, but he thinks he gonna be okay." That was good news to Luke…real good news.

Back in Blytheville, Ronnie was at Prosecutor Port's office.

"Good afternoon Ronnie. What can I do for you today?" "Hey Marshal, how was Jamaica?" "Well, I wasn't in Jamaica, I was in the Bahamas, but it was great! The weather out there this time of year is just wonderful. Got some fishing in and a whole bunch of margaritas…if you know what I mean?" Ronnie figured he knew exactly what the prosecutor was talking about.

"The reason I'm here Marshal is to talk to you about the Luther Price case. Some new evidence has come to light that I truly believe will exonerate Luther, and I would like to go over it with you."

"Well Ronnie, the prosecutor's office is always ready to listen to anything that will help a wrongly convicted man out of a fix, but I got to be honest with you,I don't believe Price is innocent, and that case, in all honesty, was the biggest case this office has had in years. I believe we had a good case against Mr. Price, and the fact that he pled guilty to the charges assures me of that all the more. However, you can feel free to show me what you have, and we will go from there."

"Fair enough," Ronnie agreed. "First of all, Buddy Wrights story does not stand up to scrutiny. I have a witness who will testify that Buddy was *not* on the boat the night of the murders as he claimed. The boat captain is sure that Wright wasn't at work that night and has time sheets and a crew roster to prove it." The prosecutor appeared to be listening intently.

"Secondly, an attendant at Scotties Truck Stop says he saw Buddy go into the restroom at the back of the station, and he says it looked like he was covered in blood. And as you well know, there was a partial print on Luke's knife that was not his, and no one seems to know who it belonged to. I will bet you it's Wrights fingerprint."

Marshal seemed to consider the information that Ronnie was giving him.

"I don't know Ronnie. It all seems to be a little too convenient to me. What about motive?" "Motive? Ronnie became a little indignant. "The dude caught Tiny going at it with his wife, man! What better motive is there than infidelity?"

Marshal was shaking his head negatively by now.

"Now Ronnie, I'm not going to put this office's reputation on the line for rumor and innuendo. This was a solid case, and I plan on standing by it. Luther Price is not going to get a new trial based on that if I have anything to say about it, and that is my final word. I'm sorry Ronnie, but that's got to be the way it is."

Ronnie sat in his car in front of the courthouse, with his head against the steering wheel. What was it that this asshole couldn't see?

"OK," Ronnie thought, "there's more than one way to skin a cat. He knew that when Governor Winthrop Rockefeller took office the year before, he had brought in a whole new crew of reformist, and that one of those new liberals was the States Attorney General.

Ronnie was just going to have to make a trip to Little Rock. That's all there was to it!

Back at Cummins, it seemed that the warden's scandal was coming to a head rather quickly.

While the new administration at the state capitol was working toward changing how business was done, one of the areas that had loomed large in the Governor's mind was the penal system in the State.

Rockefeller had known for a long time that the prison system was in big trouble, and he intended to get things straightened out in that regard, and he intended to make that his first priority. That was why he had sent investigators out to see what they could dig up...and dig shit up they would do!

Two days before Christmas 1967, at about 7:am, some inmates saw the warden, an Arkansas State Trooper, and two long line riders, loading cardboard boxes into two black Ford sedans at the warden's house, and then drive away from the unit in a very big hurry.

Thirty minutes later, those same inmates looked up the road toward the main highway, and saw a procession of vehicles headed their way.

There were six state police cars, and a school bus in the procession.

At the main gate, the parade came to a screeching halt and men in uniforms with high-powered rifles and shotguns poured out of the cars and the bus and pointed their weapons at the guard up in the tower.

One man, wearing black slacks, a white shirt, a thin tie and carrying a manila envelope stopped at the base of the guard tower and shouted up to the inmate guard manning the tower.

"You...up there...my name is Jefferson Morton, and by order of the Governor of the State of Arkansas, I command you to unlock the sally-port gate, surrender your weapons, and come down from there."

The inmate in the tower clutched the rifle to his chest and looked at the scene playing out below him, seemingly unsure about what to do. Finally he dropped the rifle to the man on the ground, turned around and pushed the gate lock button, and descended the steps to the ground.

When the guard exited the tower, the man in black nodded toward one of the State Police officers, and the cop moved forward and placed the inmate guard in handcuffs.

The uniformed police that had been on the bus then formed ranks along the barbed wire fence in front of the prison, and stood stoically with their weapons in their hands at waist level.

Another officer ascended the stairs of the tower and took up a position looking over the compound as the man in black and a handful of officers went inside.

———————————————————————

–

For the next several weeks there were many changes implemented by the new administration, including of course, breaking down the old system of inmate guards, disarming all inmates, and in general trying to completely overhaul the prison system.

It seems that the powers that be wanted to get national accreditation for their penal system; but in order for them to be able to accomplish that, they would need to bring in outside help.

The Governor of Arkansas asked for help from the state with what many consider (even to this day) the ultimate prison system…Texas.

Texas's penal system had at a time in it's long history, been in pretty much the same state of dis-array as Arkansas's, but with progressive *and* aggressive thinking, Texas had turned itself around and became a model of modern prison reform.

Not to say that Texas did not still run a tight ship, (Texas still has the dubious distinction of being the state that puts more people to death) but they ran a humane penal system that still made inmates work, but not in the brutal fashions that had been the norm for many if not all prisons around the world.

The food was better, medical care was more than adequate, and there were opportunities for rehabilitation.

That was what Rockefeller wanted for his state.

After the initial investigations, the State determined that there was more than enough evidence to bring charges against Jim Byrton, the deputy warden at Tucker, eight long line riders, four Department of Corrections officers, and more than a dozen of Byrton's cronies and partners in the outer world.

The charges ran the gamut from extortion, bribery, murder, theft of state property, prostitution and plain old theft. Jim Byrton turned himself in to authorities on July 8, 1968.

The only charge that the state could get to stick to Big Jim was the theft charges, to which Big Jim was sentence to five years in prison.

However, Jim Byrton never served one single day in prison. The judge suspended the sentence because, as he told Jim in court, "Mr. Byrton, it pains me greatly to have to suspend this sentence. You sir have brought great shame on this state; but if I sent you to jail, you would not last one single hour in your own prison, I can assure you of that!"

On August 1, 1968, The charges against Luther Dee Price were dropped, and he was freed from the Cummins Unit.

On that day, two men left prison...Luke to freedom, and Buddy Wright to the Mississippi County Jail, where he would await trial for the murders of Tiny Joe Hargett, and Mindy Wright.

During the early Fall of 1968, one hundred sixty two men were paroled from the Arkansas Department of Corrections.

Shorty and Chicken were two of them.

THE END

ABOUT THE AUTHOR

Bobby Gene Priest was born in Northeast Arkansas in 1955.

Bobby traveled the country as a young boy since his father tended to move the family around quite a lot.

He was married to Debra Lynn for over thirty-six years and they raised four daughters: April, Roseanne, Amanda and Bobbie Jean.

Bobby attended the University of Arkansas School of Architecture briefly in 1996 and 1997, and has been a private pilot, singer/songwriter, and a homebuilder and master carpenter.

Trying to feed a severe gambling addiction, Bobby made a number of bad decisions and was sentenced to 1 year in the Nevada Dept. of Corrections, and upon his release in 2006, was extradited back to his home state of Arkansas and began serving a 3- ½ year sentence, the first year spent at the Varner Unit about one mile from Cummins, and the rest of his sentence was served at the Benton Work Release Center in Saline County.

APPENDIX

If you would like to know more about the history of the Arkansas Dept, of Corrections, there are many websites to visit that will give you comprehensive information on the subject.

The author recommends you start your search at "Arkansas Dept. of Corrections" on Wikipedia

The author list a couple others here:

- http://www.encyclopediaofarkansas.net/encyclopedia/entry-detail.aspx?entryID=3485
- http://www.arkansasonline.com/news/2009/may/17/photos-cummins-window-arkansas-history/

Made in the USA
Columbia, SC
11 April 2025

56459416R00045